Andy
shoppi

Story by Maria Bird
Illustrated by Matvyn Wright

HODDER AND STOUGHTON
LONDON SYDNEY AUCKLAND TORONTO

One morning Andy Pandy looked in his cupboard, and there was nothing in it. It was quite empty. 'Won't there be anything for dinner?' asked Teddy. 'Yes,' said Andy. 'We will go to the shops and buy a lot of things.'

So they got out Andy Pandy's motor-car. Teddy fetched a big shopping bag, and put Looby Loo in the back, so that she could go too. Then Andy sat in the driving seat, and began to pedal away as fast as he could.

As soon as they got to the shops Andy Pandy left his motor-car in a safe place and told Looby Loo to look after it. Then he and Teddy took the bag, and went to a big shop that sold everything you can think of.

When they came out the bag was so full that they could hardly carry it between them. There were cakes and sausages and lettuces and milk and chocolates and jellies, and two fishes which stuck out of the top. And there was some oatmeal to make porridge for breakfast as well.

The bag was so full that there was no room in the car for it, so Andy Pandy hung it on the back. That made the car heavier than ever, and Andy had to push very hard to get it to start. As soon as it did, the fishes fell out on to the ground.

At once two little cats ran up.
'How lovely,' they said. 'We
were just wondering what
there was for dinner.' So down
they sat, and began on the
fish, purring all the time.
They were very happy cats.

After a while Andy Pandy went over a bump, and out fell the lettuces. No sooner had they landed than two rabbits saw them. 'How lovely,' they said. 'We were just wondering what there was for dinner.' So down they sat, wriggling their noses all the time. They were very happy rabbits.

Now Andy Pandy didn't know that there was a big hole in the bottom too. And as they went along, out fell the packet of oatmeal. Two hens saw it. 'How lovely,' they said. 'We were just wondering what there was for dinner.' So down they sat, pecking away busily. They were very happy hens.

By the time Andy Pandy got home, the shopping bag was empty and it was only when he had put the motor-car away, and looked at the great hole in the bag, that he knew what had happened.

'What shall we do, Teddy?' he cried. 'All our things have fallen out of the bottom of the bag.' 'Oh dear,' said Teddy. 'And I am so hungry.' 'We shall have to go back and buy some more,' said Andy Pandy. 'Have you any pennies left?' asked Teddy.

Andy Pandy looked rather sad. 'Well,' he said, 'I have. But I'll have to get it out of my piggy bank.' He looked up to the shelf where his china pig money-bank was, and it seemed to him as if the pig was looking out of the window and smiling.

He climbed on to a chair to reach the china pig, but as he did so he looked out of the window. Coming up the garden path were two little cats, each carrying a fish. He jumped down to open the door and there were two fish on the doorstep. 'Miaow,' said the little cats. 'We couldn't eat them all.'

'Well,' said Andy Pandy, 'at least we can have fish for dinner. Hurry up, Teddy, and fetch the frying pan.' Then he saw two rabbits coming up the garden path. Their noses wiggled up and down as they laid two lettuces on the doorstep. 'Wiggle, wiggle,' they said. 'We couldn't eat them all.'

No sooner had Andy Pandy said 'Thank you' than two hens came up the garden path carrying between them a packet half full of oatmeal. 'Cluck, cluck,' they clucked. 'We couldn't eat it all.' So then on the doorstep were two fishes, two lettuces and enough oatmeal to make some porridge.

'Aren't we lucky to have such kind friends?' said Andy Pandy. 'Now we shall be able to have some dinner after all, and I haven't had to take any pennies out of my piggy bank. But before we begin I'm going to get a needle and thread and sew up that hole in my shopping bag.'

Copyright 1954 Andy Pandy Ltd

ISBN 0 340 03053 4

First published 1954 by Brockhampton Press Ltd
(now Hodder and Stoughton Children's Books)
Reprinted 1987

Published by Hodder and Stoughton Children's Books,
a division of Hodder and Stoughton Ltd,
Mill Road, Dunton Green, Sevenoaks, Kent TN13 2YJ

Printed in Great Britain by Cambus Litho, East Kilbride